MOLE MUSIC

 SQUARE FISH • *Henry Holt and Company* • *New York*

MOLE MUSIC

Written and illustrated by
David McPhail

For Lisa,
and for the GANG at SWIFT—
Great job!
and special thanks to Nancy, who made the music possible

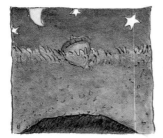  

SQUARE
FISH
An Imprint of Macmillan

Library of Congress Cataloging-in-Publication Data
McPhail, David M.
Mole music / by David McPhail.
p.   cm.
Summary: Feeling that something is missing in his simple life,
Mole acquires a violin and learns to make beautiful, joyful music.
ISBN 978-0-8050-6766-8
[1. Moles (Animals)—Fiction. 2. Violin—Fiction. 3. Music—Fiction.] I. Title.
PZ7.M4788185Mo 1999   [E]—dc21   98-21318

Originally published in the United States by Henry Holt and Company
First Square Fish Edition: June 2012
Square Fish logo designed by Filomena Tuosto
Typography by Martha Rago
The artist used watercolor and ink on illustration board to create the illustrations for this book.
mackids.com

25

AR: 2.7 / LEXILE: AD380L

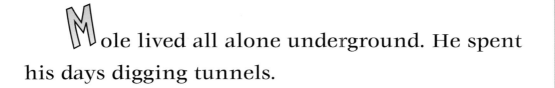ole lived all alone underground. He spent his days digging tunnels.

At night he ate his supper in front of the TV and then went to bed.

Mole liked his life, but lately he had begun
to feel there was something missing.

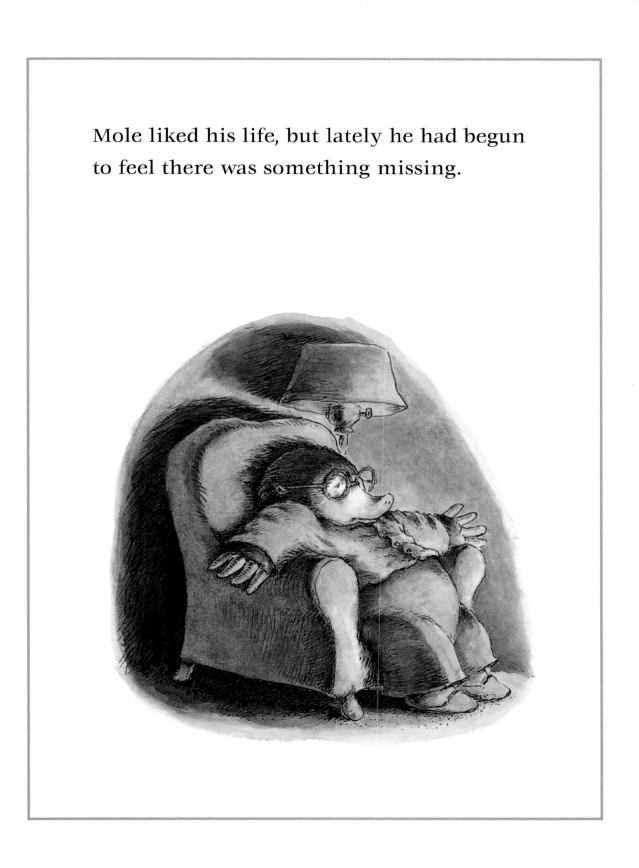

One night on the television a man played the violin. He made the most beautiful music Mole had ever heard.

"I want to make beautiful music, too,"
Mole said to himself.

So the next day he sent away for a violin
of his own.

Every day Mole checked his mailbox.

No violin.

Finally, after nearly three weeks, it arrived.

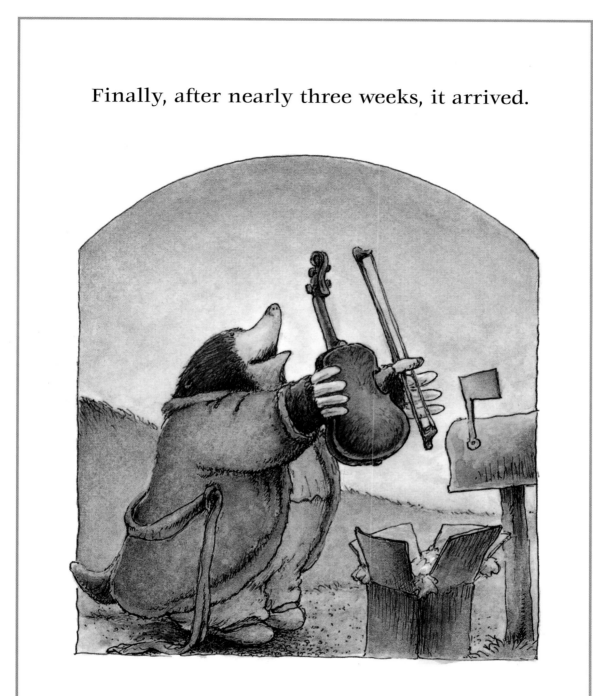

Mole was so excited.

He picked up the violin and drew the bow across the strings.

But instead of beautiful music, all he made was a horrible screeching sound.

Mole tried again.

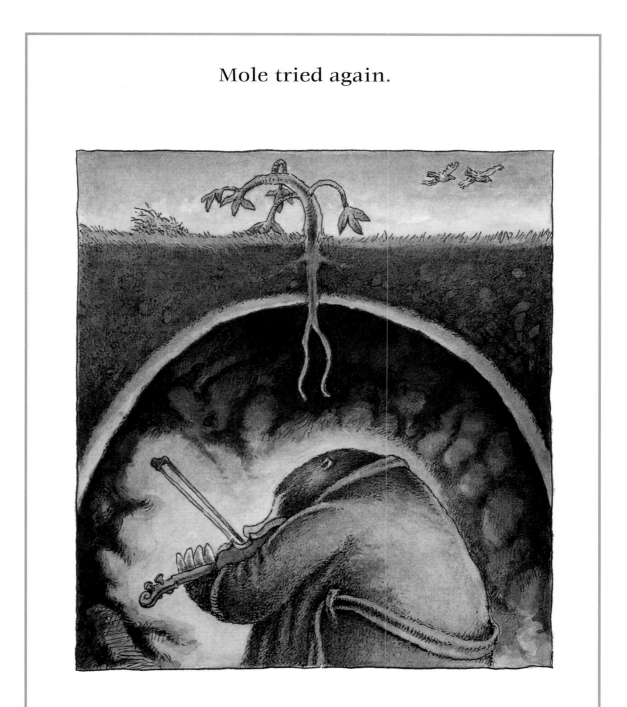

The violin still screeched, but not quite
so horribly.

Mole kept at it.

After about a week he could play one note—
then two. And before a month went by, he
could play an entire scale.

Mole continued to practice.

He learned to put the notes together in a
simple song.

Years went by.

Mole got better and better.

He was happier than he'd ever been.
During the day, as he dug tunnels,
Mole hummed the music he would
play at night.

Now Mole played even
better than the man he'd
seen on TV so long ago.

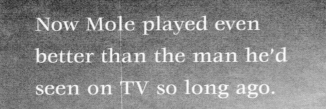

Sometimes he wondered
what it would be like to
play his music for people.

He imagined himself playing
before a huge audience.

He imagined that he played
for presidents and queens.

He even imagined that his music could reach into people's hearts and melt away their anger and sadness.

Why, maybe his music
could even change the world!

Mole laughed at himself.